Pebble® Plus

Plant Life Cycles

The Life Cycle of an Apple Tree

by Linda Tagliaferro

Consulting Editor: Gail Saunders-Smith, PhD

Consultant: Judson R. Scott, Current President
American Society of Consulting Arborists

Capstone
press®

Mankato, Minnesota

Pebble Plus is published by Capstone Press,
151 Good Counsel Drive, P.O. Box 669, Mankato, Minnesota 56002.
www.capstonepress.com

1 2 3 4 5 6 12 11 10 09 08 07

Library of Congress Cataloging-in-Publication Data
Tagliaferro, Linda.
    The life cycle of an apple tree / by Linda Tagliaferro.
    p. cm. —(Pebble Plus. Plant life cycles)
    Summary: "Simple text and photographs present the life cycle of an apple tree from seed to adult
plant"—Provided by publisher.
    Includes bibliographical references and index.
    ISBN-13: 978-0-7368-6709-2 (hardcover)
    ISBN-10: 0-7368-6709-0 (hardcover)
    1. Apples—Life cycle—Juvenile literature. I. Title. II. Series.
SB363.T23 2007
634'.11—dc22   2006020938

Editorial Credits
Sarah L. Schuette, editor; Bobbi J. Wyss, set designer; Jo Miller, photo researcher/photo editor

Photo Credits
Art Directors/Helene Rogers, 21 (blossoms)
Corbis, cover (tree)
© David Liebman Pink Guppy/Jenny Winkelman, 13; Vera Foss Bradshaw, 11
Dwight R. Kuhn, cover (seedling), 7, 19, 20 (seedling)
Getty Images Inc./Photonica/Keith Goldstein, 21 (apples)
Index Stock Imagery/Lynn Stone, 17
Shutterstock/Andriy Doriy, 20 (apple slice); Neil Webster, cover (soil)
Unicorn Stock Photos/Gary Randall, cover (apple half), 5; M. Siluk, 15
Visuals Unlimited/Dick Thomas, 9

Note to Parents and Teachers

The Plant Life Cycles set supports national science standards related to the life cycles
of plants and animals. This book describes and illustrates the life cycle of an apple tree.
The images support early readers in understanding the text. The repetition of words and
phrases helps early readers learn new words. This book also introduces early readers
to subject-specific vocabulary words, which are defined in the Glossary section. Early
readers may need assistance to read some words and to use the Table of Contents,
Glossary, Read More, Internet Sites, and Index sections of the book.

Table of Contents

Apple Seeds

How do apple trees grow?

Apple trees grow

from tiny apple seeds.

You can find apple seeds

inside apples.

Apple seeds need sunlight,
soil, water and warmth.
Then they sprout and grow.

Growing

Apple trees have one main stem called the trunk. Branches grow on the trunk. Leaves cover the tree.

After three years,

flower buds form

and open in summer.

Apple blossoms fill

the whole tree.

11

Parts of the flower blossoms
turn into fruit.
The little green apples keep
growing bigger.
Seeds form inside.

Apples!

Apples grow all summer
and turn red in fall.
They are ripe
and ready to be picked.

Some apples fall
to the ground.
They rot and the seeds
come out.

Starting Over

Next year, new apple trees can grow from the seeds. The life cycle continues.

How Apple Trees Grow

seeds

young tree

blossoms

apples

21

Glossary

life cycle—the stages in the life of a plant that include growing, reproducing, and dying

seed—the part of a flowering plant that can grow into a new plant

soil—the dirt where plants grow; most plants get their food and water from the soil.

sprout—to grow, appear, or develop quickly; sprouting seeds produce roots and stems.

stem—the long main part of a plant that makes leaves

trunk—the main stem of a tree

Read More

Bauer, David. *My Apple Tree.* Mankato, Minn.: Yellow Umbrella Books, 2006.

Ganeri, Anita. *From Seed to Apple.* How Living Things Grow. Chicago: Heinemann, 2006.

Mattern, Joanne. *How Apple Trees Grow.* How Plants Grow. Milwaukee: Weekly Reader Early Learning Library, 2006.

Internet Sites

FactHound offers a safe, fun way to find Internet sites related to this book. All of the sites on FactHound have been researched by our staff.

Here's how:

1. Visit *www.facthound.com*

2. Choose your grade level.

3. Type in this book ID **0736867090** for age-appropriate sites. You may also browse subjects by clicking on letters, or by clicking on pictures and words.

4. Click on the **Fetch It** button.

FactHound will fetch the best sites for you!

Index

Word Count: 128
Grade: 1
Early-Intervention Level: 14